TOWN DOG

Carolyn Bear

Illustrated by
Scoular Anderson

OXFORD
UNIVERSITY PRESS

OXFORD
UNIVERSITY PRESS

Great Clarendon Street, Oxford, OX2 6DP,
United Kingdom

Oxford University Press is a department of the University of Oxford.
It furthers the University's objective of excellence in research, scholarship,
and education by publishing worldwide. Oxford is a registered trade mark of
Oxford University Press in the UK and in certain other countries

Text © Carolyn Bear 2003

The moral rights of the author have been asserted

First published in this edition 2016

British Library Cataloguing in Publication Data
Data available

978-0-19-837721-4

7 9 10 8

Paper used in the production of this book is a natural, recyclable product
made from wood grown in sustainable forests. The manufacturing process
conforms to the environmental regulations of the country of origin.

Printed in India by Manipal Technologies Limited

Acknowledgements
Cover and inside illustrations by Scoular Anderson
Inside cover notes written by Sasha Morton

Contents

Shopping for
Lou-Lou
1 packet
dog biscuits

3 tins
chicken in
gravy

1 bone

Chapter 1
Clever Dog

The Town Dog lived with a Little Old Lady.

The Little Old Lady loved her. She let the Town Dog sleep on her bed and sit on her lap like a cat.

The Town Dog, whose name was
Lou-Lou, had a coat to wear when
it was cold.

And when it rained, the Little Old Lady
let her ride in her shopping trolley. Lou-Lou
liked to hide in the trolley.

Then she would pop out from under the shopping and make people jump.

Lou-Lou was a very clever dog. She had some important jobs to do.

She had to bark when the Little Old Lady didn't hear the doorbell.

She had to warn the Little Old Lady when something was burning in the kitchen.

And she had to clean up any food that fell on the floor.

When the Little Old Lady lost
things, like her keys or her purse,
all she had to do was say "keys"
or "purse" and Lou-Lou would run
and find them.

Then the Little Old Lady would
give her treats.

Lou-Lou really was the happiest dog
in the world.

One day something terrible happened.
The Little Old Lady had a fall and broke
her leg and was carried off to hospital.
Lou-Lou wasn't allowed to go in the
ambulance with her.

She was left all alone in the house with a dish of food and a bowl of water. She couldn't sleep all night. She didn't eat the food. She was very sad and very worried.

She thought she would never see the Little Old Lady again.

Chapter Two
Lou-Lou's New Home

The next day, a man in a uniform came and opened the front door without even ringing the doorbell. He had a cap with 'Animal Rescue' on it.

Lou-Lou barked and barked. She even growled — which surprised her. It was something she didn't know she could do.

The man put Lou-Lou in a basket and carried her out to a van. She whined and scratched at the basket. Was she being kidnapped?

But the man took her to a train station. Then he put her on a train with lots of parcels and sacks and bicycles. Doors slammed and the train started off.

Lou-Lou's basket rocked in time with the train. *Dig-a-dig-rick, dig-a-dig-rick, rick-a-rick-rick-rick, duggedy-duggedy-duggedy.*

Lou-Lou whimpered miserably. But no one came. At last she dropped off to sleep.

The next thing she knew, the train had stopped.

Her basket was lifted up and carried out of the train.

She sniffed the air. It didn't smell
at all like the town. There were interesting
animal smells and strange, scary smells
she'd never smelled before.

Her basket was handed to a man
who was waiting on the platform. He
was wearing boots covered with mud.
Lou-Lou crouched down in her basket
with her ears back. Where was he taking
her?

He put the basket in the back of a car.
There was a woman in the front and a
Terrible Child strapped into a baby seat in
the back.

The Terrible Child was screaming and
the woman was trying to make it quiet by
waving a toy at it.

Further back, behind bars, there were two huge and fierce-looking dogs. They barked at Lou-Lou with deep, hollow barks.

The Terrible Child stopped crying when he saw Lou-Lou. He poked his hand into her basket and tried to pull her tail.

After a long and bumpy journey,
they arrived at a farm. The man and the
woman climbed out of the car. They took
the Terrible Child out of the baby seat and
opened the back of the car to let out the
big dogs.

Then they picked up Lou-Lou's basket
and said, "Out you go."

Lou-Lou jumped out straight into
a puddle. Rain was soaking through her
fur and the wind was icy. She had to walk
along a horrible, muddy track with the
other dogs.

Lou-Lou walked on tiptoe and
jumped over the puddles. The other dogs
didn't mind getting wet and dirty and
they barked at Lou-Lou in a jeering way.

When they reached the house, all the dogs were taken into a back room with a cold stone floor and given bowls of dog food.

There were two cats there, too, and they came and sniffed Lou-Lou, to find out if she was a cat.

Lou-Lou barked to make sure they knew she was a dog. They backed away and Lou-Lou was glad.

Lou-Lou was very hungry, but she didn't eat her dinner. She jumped back into her basket and tried to go to sleep.

It was a freezing night, and very dark outside. Animals she didn't know made strange and frightening noises. The other two dogs slept on the stone floor and snored and didn't seem to care.

Lou-Lou lay awake thinking of the
saucer of hot chocolate and the dog biscuit
that she used to have at home with
the Little Old Lady.

When at last she fell asleep, she
dreamed she was riding in a shopping
trolley full of big, juicy bones.

Chapter Three
Lou-Lou Feels Ashamed

The next day, the man came in wearing his boots. He took the other two dogs with him and went out into the fields.

That's when Lou-Lou heard this terrible "MOOOO!" outside. It was followed by a lot more even louder MOOOOS!

Lou-Lou was so frightened she buried
herself in a basket of washing. When the
woman came to do the ironing, she found
Lou-Lou. She was really angry.

Lou-Lou felt ashamed. She sat
quietly in a corner and watched the
Terrible Child.

The Terrible Child threw a lot of food and toys around and then he went to sleep. When he woke up again, he threw a lot more food and then started chasing Lou-Lou around the room.

That's when she discovered that she could jump out through the cat flap.

That night, the two dogs came back
with the man.

The two dogs were covered with mud
and smelled as if they had rolled in
something horrible. They growled at
Lou-Lou and she tried to get as far away
from them as she could.

She jumped on to the woman's lap.
The woman wasn't a bit like the Little
Old Lady. She pushed Lou-Lou off.

Then the man said he was going to
teach Lou-Lou how to behave like a
proper dog.

Chapter Four
Lucky Escape

For the next week, Lou-Lou had a terrible time. She didn't want to learn how to behave like a dog. For a start, she had to spend all day outside, even when it was raining. Her tail was down and her ears were back all the time.

The other dogs just laughed at her
and showed off. They didn't want to
play with her.

There were some huge animals in
the fields that she hadn't seen before.
At first, Lou-Lou thought they were dogs.
But they didn't smell like dogs and they
didn't bark.

She went to take a closer look. One of them was bigger than the others. When he saw Lou-Lou he rolled his eyes and snorted.

He had huge, sharp horns. He lowered his head and pawed the ground. He was a bull.

Lou-Lou started backing away. Then she started running. She could hear the bull thundering after her. She ran as fast as her four legs would take her.

She shot through a gap in the hedge just as the bull was about to toss her in the air.

After that, Lou-Lou decided it would be best to play with smaller animals. She even tried to make friends with the cats. One of their favourite games was chasing each other around the house and garden, in and out through the cat flap. Lou-Lou joined in.

The two big dogs looked on in disgust.

"A dog going through a cat flap," said one of them, and laughed in a nasty way. The other dog sniggered. Lou-Lou felt very ashamed.

Chapter Five
To the Rescue

Then, early one morning, the woman took the man to catch the train. Lou-Lou was sitting in the back of the car. She wondered where he was going.

When the woman got back she started to clean the whole house.

When she had finished cleaning,
she set the table with a tablecloth and the
best china.

The dogs were told to stay outside so
that they didn't make muddy pawprints
everywhere.

But Lou-Lou crept in through the cat
flap. She hid under the table.

Lou-Lou watched as the woman got the Terrible Child ready in his outdoor clothes. Then the woman took a rug out to the car.

But the minute that she was outside, the Terrible Child toddled across the floor and slammed the front door shut. Lou-Lou was locked in – and so was the Terrible Child!

The Terrible Child then walked
over to the table and pulled at the
tablecloth.

All the tea cups and saucers and
plates and spoons and jam and milk
went sliding with a terrible crash on to
the floor. Lou-Lou was shocked.

The woman was now peering through the letterbox.

She called out, "Don't do that! Come to Mummy."

But the Terrible Child took no notice. He went over to the fireplace and started throwing things into the fire.

A magazine slid out of the fire on to the rug. A thin wisp of flame started to dart across the floor.

The woman was screaming. She was desperate. She could see her keys on the table, but couldn't get to them.

"Keys," she shouted to the Terrible Child. "Bring the keys to Mummy."

Lou-Lou pricked up her ears. "Keys!"

The Terrible Child didn't understand. The other two dogs stared through the window helplessly. The cats were trying to climb up the curtains.

All the animals were terrified.
They didn't know what to do.

Lou-Lou spotted the keys lying on
the table. Quick as a flash, she jumped
up on a chair and grasped the keys in
her mouth. Then she dashed out
through the cat flap. She gave the keys
to the woman.

The woman unlocked the door, raced
into the room, threw the rug over the
flames and put them out. She picked
up the Terrible Child and hugged him.
She was crying. Then she turned to
Lou-Lou.

"Oh, you good dog," she said, blowing her nose.

"What a clever dog you are," she said, wiping her eyes. She lifted Lou-Lou up and hugged her, too.

The other dogs looked at Lou-Lou with respect.

Lou-Lou felt so proud.

Chapter Six
Home Again

The woman made sure that the fire
was well and truly out and cleared up
the mess on the floor. Then she bundled
the Terrible Child and Lou-Lou into
the car and drove off at a very fast
pace.

The Terrible Child was quiet for once.
He stroked Lou-Lou nicely and said "Doc-
Duc," which was the nearest he could get
to "Good dog."

Soon they arrived at the train
station. The woman got out of the car
and took the Terrible Child and Lou-Lou
with her.

They went on to the platform and
waited for the train to come. Lou-Lou
expected they were waiting for the man.

And sure enough, as the train came
in, there he was, waving through the
window.

He climbed out of the train. Then a guard came and helped him carry something heavy out of the train. It was a wheelchair and sitting in it, who should it be but the Little Old Lady, with her leg all done up in a big plaster cast!

Lou-Lou could not believe her eyes. She leaped up and tried to lick the Little Old Lady's face.

Then the woman told the man how clever Lou-Lou had been. After that, she was allowed to ride back home on the Little Old Lady's lap.

Lou-Lou stayed in the country until the Little Old Lady's leg got better.

While they were in the country, nobody tried to make her behave like a dog any more. They let her stay inside in the warm and sit with the Little Old Lady.

The other dogs didn't laugh or snigger at her, either. They looked up to her with respect.

About the author

The idea for writing this book came from a real dog. Her owner couldn't look after her any more in the city, so she came to live with us in the country.

The first time she saw a cow she came back through the hedge with her eyes as big as saucers. She wouldn't go out in the rain and used to tip-toe around the puddles. But she's a very intelligent dog. With time, she's got used to country life. She's sitting beside me now and looks as if she'd like to add a word or two herself if only she could type.